For Noemi, with thanks
for giving me the idea – AS

First published in Great Britain in 2006 by Bloomsbury Publishing Plc
38 Soho Square, London, W1D 3HB

Text copyright © Antonie Schneider 2005
Illustrations copyright © Helga Bansch 2005
English translation by Alyson Cole

A CIP catalogue record of this book is available from the British Library

ISBN 0 7475 8184 3
9780747581840

Printed and bound in China by South China Printing Co.

1 3 5 7 9 10 8 6 4 2

All papers used by Bloomsbury Publishing are natural, recyclable products made from wood
grown in well-managed forests. The manufacturing processes conform to the environmental
regulations of the country of origin.

Antonie Schneider
Helga Bansch

Leo's Dream

Translated by Alyson Cole

BLOOMSBURY
CHILDREN'S
BOOKS

This is Leo and his family.

Leo's mum is always very busy.

Leo's dad is always very busy too.

So it's Leo's sister, Alma, who looks after Leo.

Alma takes Leo wherever he needs to go:

to school …

    to his piano lessons …

      skiing …

        to the library …

          everywhere!

Mum never has any time for Leo. She's always in a hurry –
running to catch a train or jump in a taxi.
When Mum goes away, she calls Leo and asks, 'How are you?'
'Fine,' Leo replies.
'The sun is shining here,' says Mum.
'It's raining here,' says Leo.

One day, Leo was stuck in his room all by himself.
It was Leo's birthday the next day, and his mum had
to go to work.
He was very angry and very sad.

'You never have any time for me!' Leo shouted at his mum.
'Not even on my birthday!'
Leo sulked. He was as bitter as a lemon.

Leo began drawing on a piece of paper.
First he drew a goose. '*Mum* is a silly goose,'
Leo murmured.
Next he drew his dad as a crocodile and, finally,
a rabbit that looked like Alma.
Then he thought out loud, 'Wouldn't it be nice if
Mum, Dad and Alma really *were* all animals?'
Leo closed his eyes. He wasn't sure for
how long …

Then Leo heard a strange noise coming from the bathroom.
It sounded just like a goose honking.
Cautiously, Leo peeped around the door. He was right!
There was a goose splashing about in the bath!
And a crocodile was sitting on the loo stretching
to see himself in the mirror.
Leo could hardly believe it!
Was that his mum and dad?
Where was Alma?

'Alma!' Calling loudly, Leo ran to the kitchen. And there, sitting under the table, was a white rabbit with floppy ears, crying.
'Alma, is that you?' Leo whispered.
The rabbit nodded sadly.
'Come on,' Leo said, trying to cheer her up. 'Let's go and find Mum and Dad.'

Suddenly, the doorbell rang. It was a policeman.

'Where are your parents?' he boomed.

'My parents aren't here at the moment,' replied Leo, turning bright red. But the policeman didn't notice.

'A neighbour has reported that she saw a crocodile through your window. Crocodiles need permits, you know. I shall have to come in and investigate.'

Leo nodded, then he led the policeman through the house, his heart beating faster and faster.

In Leo's room, Alma sat so still that the policeman
thought she was a toy.
'What a lovely rabbit you have there,' he said. 'It almost
looks real.'
Luckily he didn't see the crocodile's tail or the goose's
beak under the chair.
'Your neighbour must have made a mistake,' said the
policeman, and he left.

By this time, everyone was hungry, and so Leo prepared a meal for all of them.

Carrots for Alma, sweetcorn for Mum and chicken for Dad.
Leo set the table on the floor, and everyone began to eat.
'You look so funny, Dad, with your enormous mouth!'
said Leo, laughing. Dad laughed too.
'That was delicious, Leo,' said Mum.
And Dad and Alma agreed.

When it was time for bed, Mum put her big white wings around Leo. Dad snuggled in nice and close. Then Alma cuddled up, and they listened as Mum told them a story. One by one they all fell asleep in Leo's room.

When Leo woke the next morning, all the animals had disappeared. But the piece of paper with his drawings on was still by the bed.

There was a knock at Leo's door. Then Mum, Dad and Alma appeared with a big birthday cake for Leo.

'Happy birthday to you … !' they sang.

'You didn't go away!' Leo was surprised.

'No,' Mum said. 'I wanted to celebrate your birthday with you, of course! And we all had a very funny dream last night …'

'You too …?' asked Leo, smiling.